Amanda's First Day of School

Story and Pictures by
Joan Elizabeth Goodman

A GOLDEN BOOK · NEW YORK
Western Publishing Company, Inc., Racine, Wisconsin 53404

"Wake up," said Amanda. "We have to get ready. It's my first day of school!"

"It's too early," said Mama.

"Go back to sleep," said Papa.

But Amanda was much too excited to sleep. "Today is my first day of school," she told her doll as she slipped on her new jumper. "My very *first* day of school!"

"A special breakfast for a special day," said Mama.
She gave Amanda a bowl full of blackberries
floating in honey and cream.

Amanda took two bites. "All done," she said.
"Let's go."

"Slow down," said Mama. "You can't start school
on an empty stomach."

Amanda picked at the blackberries until it was finally time to leave for school.

"Good-by, scholar," said Papa, giving Amanda a big hug.

"Good-by," said Amanda, and she raced out the door.

The schoolyard was crowded when Amanda and
Mama got there.

"School wasn't this big when we came here in the
summer," said Amanda.

"It's the same as it was in the summer," said
Mama, "only now all the teachers and students
are here."

"It looks bigger," said Amanda. "I think it grew."
And she squeezed Mama's paw.

"It's bigger inside, too," said Amanda. "The hall got longer."

"It's just the same," said Mama. "Here's your classroom. Remember the blue door?"

"No," said Amanda. "This must be the wrong school. Let's go home."

But Mama opened the classroom door.
"Welcome to school," said Miss Barron, the
teacher. "Come in, Amanda, come in!"

Amanda looked around the bustling room. Some cubs were building block caves. Some watched the ant farm with their mothers. Two boy cubs were pushing and shoving. A girl cub held on to her father and cried. It was *so* busy and *so* noisy. There were *so* many bears.

"I don't like school," said Amanda. "I want to go home."

"Please give it a chance," said Mama. "I think you will like school very much."

"And I think so, too," said Miss Barron. "School is fun. Soon we will all play a singing game together. But now come and meet Becky. She will be your partner at the yellow table."

Becky was hiding behind her father. She peeked out at Amanda.

"It's time for me to go now," said Mama.

"I'll come with you," said Amanda.

"No," said Mama. "You stay here and make friends. I'll be waiting for you when school is over. Be good, my little one."

"Now what do I do?" thought Amanda when
Mama had gone. All the other cubs were busy
building, climbing, drawing, and playing.

Amanda and Becky were the only ones not
joining in.

Becky stood by the craft table, crying softly.
Amanda felt like crying, too.
"I want to go home," said Becky. "I hate school."
"Me, too," Amanda said.

Then it was time for the singing game. Amanda and Becky stood next to each other in the big circle.

"We will sing 'The Field Folks' Song' to begin the first day of school," said Miss Barron.

Everyone had a special part. But when Miss
Barron pointed to her, Amanda forgot what she
was supposed to sing. The whole class was
watching and waiting. Someone started to giggle.
Amanda felt awful.

"You're a bee," whispered Becky. "Buzz!"

"Buzz," sang Amanda, "buzz, buzz, *buzz*!" When
her part was over, Amanda smiled at Becky.

After the song, Amanda sat down next to Becky at the yellow table. Miss Barron handed out paper and crayons.

"Now draw your song animals," she said.

Amanda drew a bee on a pink flower.

"Do you like bees?" asked Becky.

"Well... they're okay," said Amanda. "But I *love* honey!"

"Me, too!" said Becky. "Let's call our group 'The Honey Bunch.'"

"That's bee-u-tiful," said Amanda.

"Buzz, buzz, *buzz!*" said Becky.

All the other cubs laughed.

After cleanup, Miss Barron read the class a story about ten turtles that lived in the mud.

"How many turtles were there?" asked Miss Barron.

"One, two, three, four, five, six, seven, eight, nine, ten turtles!" said the class.

At rest time, Amanda and Becky shared a mat.
"Buzz," whispered Amanda.
"Buzz, buzz, *buzz!*" said Becky.
"Be still, busy bees," said Miss Barron. "Now it is *rest* time."

"Now get up and stretch," said Miss Barron. "Let's play follow-the-leader. Everyone will have a chance to be leader."

When it was Amanda's turn, she had the class flap their arms and buzz like bees. Everyone buzzed and laughed. Miss Barron laughed the loudest.

Then the bell rang. "Time to go home!" Miss Barron said.

"How was school?" asked Mama.

"First it was awful," said Amanda. "But then we got to be busy bees, and it was great." She smiled and waved to Becky. "Buzz, buzz, buzz!" she said. "See you tomorrow."